This book has been purchased
with funds from the
**St. Albert
Community Lottery Board**
for the
**Lifelong Learning Book Collection
1998 - 2000**

What Happened to the Mammoths?

Scientists Probe 12 Animal Mysteries

What Happened to the Mammoths?

and Other Explorations of Science in Action

Jack Myers, Ph.D.
Senior Science Editor
HIGHLIGHTS FOR CHILDREN

Illustrated by John Rice

Boyds Mills Press

Photo credits: Page 35: Courtesy of Dr. Peter Dodson; 47: R. Blakemore.

Illustration and graphic artwork credits: Pages 12-13: Based on data of Terrie M. Williams; 24: Based on data of Mark W. J. Ferguson; 32: based on a drawing from *Weddell Seal, Consummate Diver* by G.L. Kooyman; Page 47: Based on a drawing published by *Nature*, November 27, 1997 (volume 390, page 375); 50-51: Courtesy of Robert Fox, Stephen W. Lehmkuhle, and David W. Westendorf.

Published by Caroline House
Boyds Mills Press, Inc.
A Highlights Company
815 Church Street
Honesdale, Pennsylvania 18431
Printed in China
Visit our website at: www.boydsmillspress.com

U.S. Cataloging-in-Publication Data
 (Library of Congress Standards)

Myers, Jack.

What happened to the mammoths? : and other explorations of science in action /
by Jack Myers ; illustrated by John Rice. —1st ed.
[64]p. : col. ill. ;   cm.
Includes bibliographic references and index.
Summary: Intriguing questions about animals are answered by scientists in these twelve explorations taken from the award-winning column in *Highlights for Children* magazine.
ISBN 1-56397-801-6
1. Science—Miscellanea—Juvenile literature. 2. Animals—Miscellanea Juvenile literature. 3. Questions and answers—Juvenile literature. [1. Science. 2. Animals. 3. Questions and answers.] I. Rice, John, ill. II. Title.
591 —dc21   2000   AC   CIP
99-65422

First edition, 2000
The text of this book is set in 13-point Berkeley.

10 9 8 7 6 5 4 3 2 1

CONTENTS

Introduction

Science is the search for understanding of our world. All the fun and excitement is in the search. That's where the action is. That's why this series is called Science in Action. It tells about explorations and discoveries as they happened.

All of these explorations have appeared in *Highlights for Children*. Earlier they were called Science Reporting. That was also a good title because each is based on an original and current report cited on page 62.

Most of these chapters tell about the scientific detective work that gave us answers to some great questions of pure curiosity. In some cases, new findings were made since my account was published in *Highlights*. I have updated and revised them as needed.

The illustrations are by John Rice, who has had long experience in picturing wildlife in natural settings. At the beginning of most chapters, he has slipped in just-for-fun illustrations to tell something about the ideas of the articles. Then his main illustrations will help you think about the animals themselves.

This volume contains discoveries about animals, their behavior, and the parts they play in nature. Please follow with me in the tracks of the scientists who made the discoveries.

Jack Myers

Jack Myers, Ph.D.
Senior Science Editor
Highlights for Children

Dolphins Catch a Wave

Sometimes they would rather surf than swim.

As a swimming instructor, Terrie Williams taught people how to be better swimmers. That means swimming with less effort. Anyone can thrash around in the water. It's only with training and practice that you learn to swim smoothly and with least effort. But there is a limit even for trained swimmers. Terrie couldn't help wondering why even champion swimmers have to work so hard at it. Animals that live in the water seemed to swim more easily. What makes them better swimmers?

Terrie started in to make like a scientist and study swimming animals. She studied sea otters, seals, and sea lions. She has reported some surprising results about dolphins. Except for the fish, dolphins seem to be world-champion swimmers.

In order to compare animals as swimmers, it is important to know how fast they are swimming. You know that swimming across the pool as fast as you can takes a lot more energy than when you just lazily swim across. So measuring swimming speed is important.

In Hawaii there is a laboratory where for many years dolphins have been studied right out in the ocean. They have been taught to obey commands given by underwater sounds. So it was easy for Terrie to teach two dolphins to swim alongside a motorboat going at a measured speed.

The Dolphin's Energy

Terrie wanted to find out how fast the dolphins were spending energy as they swam alongside the boat. The standard way to measure energy use by an animal is to measure how fast it uses oxygen. That tells how fast food is being burned in the body.

But Terrie had a problem. There was no way she could measure oxygen use by a dolphin swimming out in the ocean beside a motorboat.

Terrie solved the problem in a way that we scientists often use. Very often we can't measure exactly what we want to know about. Then we try to find something else we *can* measure that will tell us about what we want to know.

Terrie found that she could measure the rate of a dolphin's heartbeat. Small metal plates held against the skin by a tight harness were used to pick up the strong electrical signal that goes with each heartbeat. Then she trained the dolphins to push a raft in an area where she could measure both heart rate and rate of oxygen uptake at the same time. As the dolphins pushed harder, the heart rate and oxygen rate went up together. So with just a little math, Terrie could use heart rate to measure the rate of energy used by a swimming dolphin.

Now Terrie was ready to ask questions about dolphins and their rate of energy use at different swimming speeds.

In the first experiment, a signal was given for the dolphin to swim alongside the motorboat in position A shown in the drawing on pages 12 and 13. The boat speed was held at 5 miles per hour (MPH). Then the dolphin was spending energy at a rate of about one-half horsepower (HP). That's only a little greater than a dolphin spends energy just resting. So the speed of 5 MPH is like a cruising speed—one that the dolphin can keep up all day.

You might like to compare the dolphin to a human swimmer. It just happens that the dolphin's cruising speed is almost the same as the world record for human swimmers in the 100-meter freestyle. In order to swim at that speed, a person has to spend energy at a rate of almost $2\frac{1}{2}$ HP. You can see that humans are very poor swimmers compared to dolphins. We have to spend energy five times faster.

There were other experiments at greater speeds. When the speed was increased to $6\frac{1}{2}$ MPH, the dolphin had to work a lot harder and its energy rate became about $1\frac{1}{2}$ HP. Then the boat speed was raised to $8\frac{1}{2}$ MPH. That must be faster than a dolphin likes to swim for any long distance

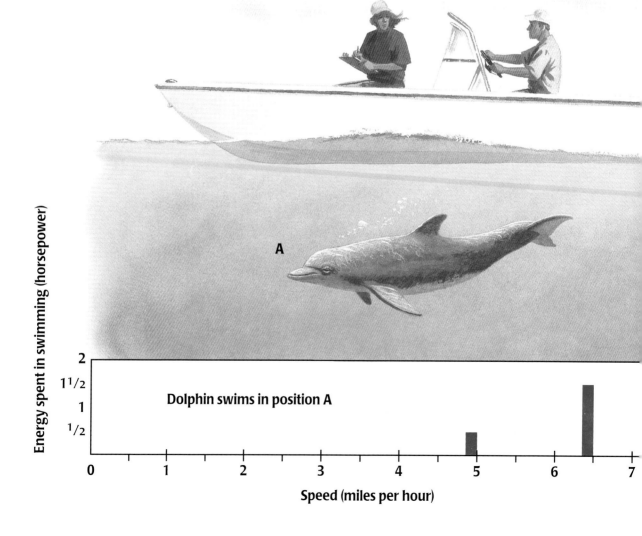

Dolphin swims in position A

because there was nothing Terrie could do to make a dolphin stay in position beside the boat. The dolphin would always drift back to position B in the little wave or wake of the boat. It was wave-riding.

When a dolphin sneaked into position B in the wake, it stayed close to the surface and appeared almost motionless. Even though it was moving faster, its energy rate went back down to about 1 HP. No one knows exactly how the dolphin does it. But there is no doubt that it has a way of getting help from the wave just behind the boat.

Many people who have watched dolphins tag along in the wakes of ships have thought they were just being playful. Terrie has shown that there is a better explanation. Dolphins have learned that wave-riding in the wake is an easy way to travel.

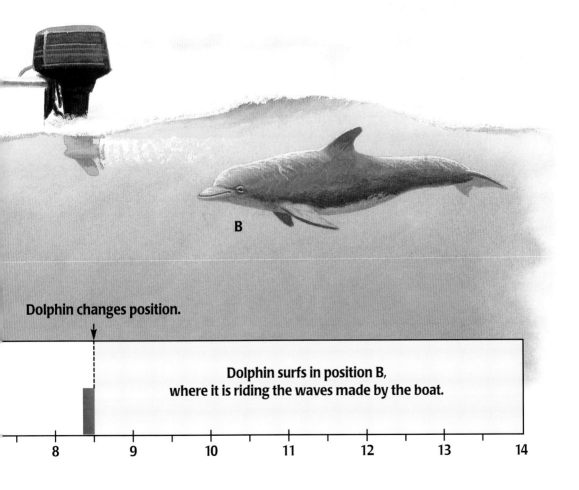

Dolphin changes position.

Dolphin surfs in position B, where it is riding the waves made by the boat.

8 9 10 11 12 13 14

B

How Cats Purr

They use their vocal cords to do both: meow and purr.

Cats have been living as our pets for many thousands of years. You might think that we would have learned all there was to know about cats long ago. Not quite. How do cats purr? Until scientists studied cats' vocal chords, that was a mystery.

As far as we know, every kind of cat can purr, even big cats like lions and tigers. Of course you and I—and most animals—can't purr. So how do the cats do it? I found an answer in a report written by medical scientists.

When a cat purrs, it seems to vibrate all over. You can feel the purr by putting your hand against the cat's body. This vibration makes the purr even more mysterious. Where is the purr made? Does it come from the cat's throat or from its chest?

By pressing a small microphone against different places on the body, the scientists found that the greatest vibrations were at its throat and right over its *larynx* (LAR-inks), or voice box. That's where the sound is made. By listening with the microphone near different places, scientists were able to show that the purr sound comes out mostly through the mouth and nose.

It's no surprise that purring should work this way, because that's how our voices work. When we talk, vibrations made in the larynx come out of the mouth as sound. You can feel the location of your larynx: Place your fingers gently against the front of your throat, then swallow or speak.

When a person speaks or a cat meows, the sounds start as vibrations of two folds of thin skinlike tissue down in the larynx. These folds, which are also called the vocal cords,

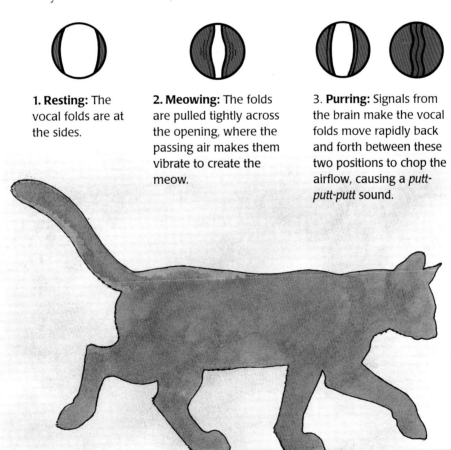

1. Resting: The vocal folds are at the sides.

2. Meowing: The folds are pulled tightly across the opening, where the passing air makes them vibrate to create the meow.

3. **Purring:** Signals from the brain make the vocal folds move rapidly back and forth between these two positions to chop the airflow, causing a *putt-putt-putt* sound.

make sounds by fluttering or vibrating in the air stream that is forced over them during speaking or meowing. They produce sound in the same way that the strings of a musical instrument do. Even though other animals don't have the gift of speech, many of them can make their vocal folds vibrate to make special sounds.

With its vocal folds, a cat can scream or meow. Scientists have looked for something separate from the vocal folds that could vibrate to make a purring sound. They couldn't find a special purring organ, and at first some of them guessed that muscles in the chest might do the job.

One Voice Box, Two Sounds

After using the microphone to find the source of the purr, the scientists knew that both the meow and the purr come from the larynx. But how can the larynx make both sounds? The scientists got clues from the differences between meowing and purring.

The first clue was that cats "speak" (or meow) only when they are breathing out, just as we do. (You can't say words very well when you are breathing in. Try it and see.) But the purr keeps on going whether the cat is breathing in or out.

A second clue was that a purr has a much lower pitch than a meow. The sounds of speaking for both cats and people are made by the vocal folds moving two hundred times a second or faster. But from the sound of purring, scientists know that is made by something that moves only about twenty-five times a second.

And a purr doesn't change in pitch as a meow does. A meow can start on a high note and end on a lower note. But a purr is always about twenty-five vibrations a minute.

Here is the strangest clue. The pitch of purring is almost the same in kittens, house cats, and big cats like cheetahs. But that seems wrong. If the sound were made by something that vibrates, the pitch should get lower as the cats get bigger. The gong of a big bell has a lower pitch than the tingle of a tiny bell, and a lion's "voice" is lower than a kitten's meow. But the lion and the kitten purr at about the

same pitch—one with a tiny larynx, and one with a king-of-the-jungle-sized larynx.

One final clue: When a cat purrs, some muscles in the larynx give electric signals that show they are flexing about twenty-five times a second.

So, the secret of purring is this: It is not caused by anything that flutters in an air stream. Instead, the moving air is pinched off into many little puffs. When a cat purrs, it has nerve messages coming from the brain to a special muscle in the larynx. That muscle swings the vocal folds together and almost closes off the air passage. Then the muscle relaxes, and the airway opens again. This pinching-and-relaxing motion, twenty-five times a second, changes the airflow from a steady stream to a *putt-putt-putt*, or *purr*.

The cat's larynx works about the same as yours does. It has muscles that can tighten the vocal folds to change how fast they vibrate as they flutter in the air stream. And, like your larynx, it has a "closing" muscle that can swing the vocal folds together to partly close off the air stream. But the cat has something more that you don't. It has a timer in its brain that can send nerve messages to the "closing" muscle at twenty-five times a second. That's why it can purr.

Try This

You can use your lips to mimic the vocal folds in making the voice sounds and the purr sounds. Hold your lips together while you blow air out. Your lips will flutter to make what some people call a "raspberry." That's like the vibrations of your vocal folds when you talk.

To mimic the purr, breathe out as you make the P sound as fast as you can, like this: *Puh-puh-puh*. That will open and close the air passage to make something like the "motorboat" sound of purring.

Alligators Get Cavities, Too

___

. . . in their eggshells.

Big alligators can be just as mean and dangerous as they look. But there is nothing scary about little alligators just starting life inside their eggshells. The shells are specially made to do the job of protecting little animals just beginning to grow. But the shell can't be too strong. After about two months of growing inside, the baby alligator must be able to break out. There is a special program that makes all this happen.

A female alligator may lay her eggs, maybe 50 or more, in a crude nest. She covers the eggs with dead leaves and mud, and splashes on water to keep the nest wet. One very good result of all this is that the decaying leaves give off a little heat and keep the eggs cozy warm. In about sixty-five days little alligators pop out of those eggs.

When alligator eggs are brought into a laboratory and cleaned up and kept warm, something goes wrong. The embryos develop all right but are never able to break out of their shells. What could cause this?

Thick Eggshells

In order to find out, a scientist studied 396 alligator eggs during this sixty-five-day incubation period. He used an electron microscope to see what happened to the eggshells. When freshly laid, the shell was about twice as thick as your fingernail and had several layers. On the outside there was a hard layer of calcium carbonate, the same stuff found in limestone. The shell is strong because it is arranged as several layers of neatly stacked crystals.

Electron-microscope pictures taken after the eggs had been incubated in a nest showed clumps of bacteria in little

pits on the surface. Each one looked as if the outer crystal layers had been dissolved away, one by one.

What will dissolve away crystals of calcium carbonate? Almost any acid. The many bacteria that cause rot and decay also produce some weak acids. One of these is carbonic acid. That's the stuff that helps to dissolve away limestone to make caves. Of course, what all of this does is to weaken the shell. By the time a little alligator is ready to hatch at sixty-five days, its shell has lots of pits in the hard outer layer. Then breaking out of the shell is no problem at all. But if the shell is kept clean, then its outer layer stays hard and is just too strong for a little alligator to break.

Study of the little pits that weaken the eggshell showed that they are formed in just about the same way that cavities are formed in your teeth. Tiny amounts of acid formed by bacteria dissolve away a hard surface layer. However, cavities in its eggshell are good for an alligator, but cavities in your teeth are bad for you.

A Surprising Thing About Alligators

Temperature has a big effect on their young.

Biologists are seldom really surprised by some new report about an animal. Most reports provide answers to well-known questions or mysteries. A few years ago I was surprised by an idea that came from a study of alligators. Here's the idea: whether a little alligator is male or female depends on how warm the egg was when it was incubating.

Why was that idea a surprise? Just because that's not the way it works in most animals. In humans, each of us has twenty-three pairs of chromosomes in almost all the cells of our bodies. When we started out, one chromosome of each pair came from each of our parents. Those chromosomes carry the thousands of messages that tell our bodies how to grow up. One particular pair determines whether a person is male or female. Just to keep track of them, biologists call these the X and Y chromosomes. And they work this way: If you have two X chromosomes (XX), you are a girl. If you have an X and a Y chromosome (XY), you are a boy. Each of us has one X and about a fifty-fifty chance of having either another X or a Y. So there is about a fifty-fifty chance of being male or female. All of this can be called a *genetic control of sex*, and it is very neat in turning out about equal numbers of males and females. Besides mammals, some reptiles, amphibians, and birds also use the XX-XY method of determining sex. I had supposed that all animals used that method. That's where the surprise came in. Alligators don't.

Turtles, Too?

Actually, scientists have been noticing that in some reptiles, especially in turtles, the temperature of eggs after they are laid in a nest seems to help determine sex. However, in the report about alligators the evidence was simple and direct.

Here is what two scientists did in studying alligators in a wildlife refuge in Louisiana. Shortly after they had been laid, a lot of eggs were gathered from alligator nests. These were put into laboratory incubators, which were set up to be as much like natural nests as possible. Six of these artificial nests were set up, each kept at a different temperature.

On page 24, you will see the results of the experiment. This graph shows the six nests and their temperatures recorded in degrees on the Celsius scale, which scientists use. It also shows the number of eggs in each nest. The scientists had only 500 eggs. They already knew that

26 degrees is too cool and 36 degrees is too warm for most alligator eggs, so they put only 50 eggs in each of those nests. The other nests in between each had 100 eggs.

Underneath the nests you can see what happened. Look at the 26-degree nest. Most of those eggs died. But of those

Temperature	26°C	28°C	30°C	32°C	34°C	36°C
Number of Eggs	50	100	100	100	100	50
Females	10	96	97	85		
Males				13	94	7
	40 died 10 females 0 males	4 died 96 females 0 males	3 died 97 females 0 males	2 died 85 females 13 males	6 died 0 females 94 males	43 died 0 females 7 males

that lived, all were females. Look at the 36-degree nest. Most of those eggs died. But of those that lived, all were males. In the nests between 28 degrees and 34 degrees most of the eggs lived, and you can see what happened to the sex of the baby alligators. Lower temperatures gave all females. A higher temperature, like 34 degrees, gave all males.

The scientists went on to do other experiments with eggs in nests out in the wilds. They put thermometers in wild nests. Nests of eggs laid on a high, dry bank were warmer. One of these at 35 degrees gave all males. Nests laid in the wet marsh were cooler. One of these at 29 degrees gave all females.

The scientists also wondered about the ratio between males and females. Is it about one-to-one as in many other animals? Over a four-year period they collected about 8,000 eggs that had incubated in their nests until almost

ready to hatch. Of the babies that hatched from those eggs there was only about 1 male for every 5 females. So that also is a lot different from what happens in most animals.

Besides the surprise in the idea, another feature of this report makes it special. There are not many scientific reports today in which you can look at the experiments, just as they were done, and figure out the results for yourself. I think you will agree with the scientists in their conclusion: The temperature of an egg during incubation determines the sex of the alligator that hatches from that egg.

Temperature and Dinosaur Eggs

Today's alligators are thought to be living relatives of the dinosaurs, which became extinct about sixty-five million years ago. There are many different ideas about why the dinosaurs disappeared rather suddenly. Now we have another idea.

Suppose that the sex of dinosaurs was determined as it is in today's alligators. And suppose that the world's climate changed just a little and became a few degrees cooler. Then all baby dinosaurs would have been females. And without any more males there never would have been any more baby dinosaurs.

Diving

How can the Weddell seal dive so deep?

Diving is a special problem. Just to keep your body working you need the steady supply of oxygen you get by breathing air.

You can't get oxygen from water the way fish do. So you try to manage on what you can carry with you. You can't stay underwater very long. But people who have had lots of practice can stay under longer.

A special group of people in Japan, the Ama, make their living by diving for fish and shellfish. Some of them may spend a total of three or four hours a day underwater. But even with all that practice, one of their dives lasts less than ninety seconds. And they need to rest and breathe between dives.

Champion Divers

Some other mammals are much better divers than we are—especially seals and whales. I'm not sure who is the grand champion, but certainly one champion must be the Weddell seal. It lives under the ice in the Antarctic. It spends much of its time under a hole in the ice where it gets its air. In search of its food, mostly fish and squid, it can make long, deep dives and then come back to its air hole.

A lot of work has been done to find out what makes the Weddell seal such a great diver. Some researchers who attached timers and depth-measuring instruments to Weddell seals found that the seal can stay down for more than an hour and sometimes goes down as deep as 2,000 feet. How can it do that? Does it have some special machinery, maybe a special way to carry oxygen?

For a number of years, Dr. Gerald Kooyman and a team of scientists studied Weddell seals in a laboratory at McMurdo Sound in Antarctica. A seal lying on the ice near its breathing hole was rolled into a big net and brought to the laboratory. A dive was simulated by putting the seal's head into a plastic box filled with seawater. To find out what was going on, the scientists made lots of measurements with instruments like those used with people in hospitals.

Big changes occurred in the seal's blood circulation. Its heart slowed down from fifty-five beats a minute to about fifteen a minute. But its blood pressure didn't change much. What happened was that most of the small blood vessels in its body pinched down and became smaller. Not much blood could flow out to the seal's skeletal muscles—the muscles of the flippers, which are like your hands and legs. Most of the blood that the heart was pumping went out only to the lungs and brain, then back again.

Pumping blood to the brain is important. The brain quits working when its oxygen supply gets low. But supplying oxygen to the brain is not as big a problem for the seal as it is for you. The seal has a lot more blood than you do—more than ten times as much—and so it has a bigger store of oxygen. But its brain is only about one-third as big as yours. Even on one of the seal's longest dives, its brain never runs short of oxygen.

But what about the skeletal muscles needed for swimming? Their blood supply is almost cut off. To understand why they still work, we need to think about how muscles work.

Muscles use a lot of energy. They get their energy by breaking down sugar in a series of chemical reactions. The very first reaction breaks down sugar into pieces called lactic acid. That first reaction goes on right in the muscle and gives it the energy to work. But it doesn't use up any oxygen at all.

Then the lactic acid must be burned, or carried away and burned someplace else in your body. It is the burning of lactic acid that takes up most of the oxygen your body uses.

The Oxygen Debt

Skeletal muscles can keep working even when they are not getting oxygen—as long as they get enough sugar and they get rid of the lactic acid. You let your muscles borrow energy that you pay back when you burn the lactic acid. It's like an energy debt you have to pay. Since you need oxygen to pay for it, that is called an *oxygen debt*.

You may have already felt the effects of oxygen debt. If you run very hard, as in a hundred-yard dash, you can't get oxygen to your muscles fast enough. They make a lot of lactic acid. That's one thing that makes your muscles get so tired. Then you will breathe rapidly and deeply for some time. You are paying back your oxygen debt.

Now let's go back to the diving seal. It has closed off most of the blood supply to its skeletal muscles. They make lots of lactic acid and give the seal a big oxygen debt. Compared to other animals, there is one thing unusual about the seal: It can handle so very much lactic acid and such a big oxygen debt.

Now you know what makes the Weddell seal a champion diver. The seal doesn't have any new or different machinery. It just has a way of managing its body machinery better—for diving.

Divers Under High Pressure

There is another problem in diving that you may have heard about. It occurs in people who dive below about 120 feet. Then air for breathing must be at high pressure. Breathing high-pressure air for very long causes problems. The first is that the diver gets woozy as a result of nitrogen poisoning. Nitrogen is the gas that makes up most of the air around us. We think of it as being inert—which it is. But at high pressure so much nitrogen dissolves in the blood and body fluids—especially in nerve tissue—that it becomes a poison.

A second part of the problem with nitrogen occurs when a diver decompresses in coming to the surface. Then a lot of the nitrogen must "undissolve." If the diver comes up quickly, the extra nitrogen comes out as bubbles that are painful and dangerous. This is the diving disease called *the bends*. To prevent it the diver must come up very slowly, so the blood can get rid of its load of nitrogen without forming bubbles.

Dr. Kooyman wondered about what happens in the Weddell seal when it dives deep-deep and stays as long as an hour. Why doesn't it have a problem with nitrogen? To find an answer, he studied seals held in a high-pressure chamber that mimicked the condition of a deep dive. He found a surprising answer to his question. Under the pressure of a deep dive, the lungs collapse until only a tiny amount of air—and nitrogen—is left in contact with the blood.

Collapse of the lung is a lot more complicated than it sounds. The lungs are not just big bags of air. Their job is to bring blood and air close together so the blood can take up oxygen and lose carbon dioxide. The lungs are a spongy tissue. The little air-carrying tubes branch and branch again until they end up in tiny sacs called *alveoli*. That's where the business of the lungs takes place between the air in the alveoli and blood flowing in little tubes around them. In your breathing, the alveoli get larger when you breathe in and smaller when you breathe out. But they are always partly filled with air and never really empty.

In thinking about collapse of the lungs in a diving seal we are really thinking about something special that happens to the alveoli. In the figure you will see diagrams of alveoli reproduced from the work of Dr. Kooyman. You can see what collapse of the lungs really means. It is a specialty of the seal (and some other diving animals) that is still not completely understood. It is something that never happens in your lungs but happens in the lungs of a Weddell seal every day.

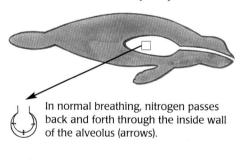

Unlike a human, the Weddell seal can dive for long periods without becoming sick from either nitrogen poisoning or the bends. These illnesses are caused by long dives, when too much nitrogen gas from the air can be dissolved into the blood. The seal's secret is that its lungs can collapse, pushing out most of the air, including nitrogen. The lungs carry less nitrogen, so less is dissolved into the blood. These drawings show how one of the lung's many tiny air sacs (alveoli) collapses.

In normal breathing, nitrogen passes back and forth through the inside wall of the alveolus (arrows).

In diving, increasing water pressure squeezes air out of the alveolus.

In a long, deep dive, the alveolus collapses completely with no air inside

The Dinosaur That Came Home

After millions of years, Ava resurfaced in Montana.

It was not a very big dinosaur, not one of those scary, meat-eating kinds. We will call it Ava because that's part of the name that scientists would give it almost eighty million years after it died. If you could have seen it munching on plants along the river's edge, you would have thought that it looked happy and rather friendly. But that quiet scene didn't last.

Farther up the river a sudden thunderstorm had filled the valley with water. A flash flood came down the river as a wall of water. It carried along trees and rocks and sand—and Ava. Not even a very large dinosaur could have survived.

At a sharp bend in the river, trees and rocks and Ava all became tangled together and wedged against the bank.

When the rest of the flood finally went by, Ava's body lay buried under sand and mud. In less than a year its soft parts had decayed, leaving only the bones.

Fossils Locked in Stone

Years went by, millions and millions of years. Minerals from the soil filtered into Ava's bones and turned them into rock-hard fossils. Mountains rose, and water no longer flowed into the old river. And the sand gradually hardened into a brown sandstone surrounding everything that the flood had once swept together.

As more millions of years went by, wind and rain wore down and smoothed out what had once been hills and valleys. In time, parts of Ava's rock-hard skeleton began to stick out above the surface.

Dr. Peter Dodson is a professor in the School of Veterinary Medicine at the University of Pennsylvania. His student Anthony Fiorello aided in digging out Ava and many other fossils. Another student, Paul Pankalski, made the replica of Ava's skeleton.

In 1981 Eddie and Ava Cole found some of the dinosaur's fossilized bones on the Careless Creek Ranch near Harlowton, Montana. Getting out the fossils was a job for dinosaur scientists.

Dr. Peter Dodson led the team that did the work. The digging—mostly chipping away at the surrounding sandstone—was done in the summers because many members of the team were students. They lived in tents. Water was trucked in by the Lammers family, who owned the ranch and helped as they could. It was a hot, dry job.

The hard work paid off. Ava's fossil bones turned out to be the most complete horned dinosaur skeleton ever found in Montana. It was the first of its species ever found. Dr. Dodson gave it the name *Avaceratops lammersi*. The first name honors one of the finders. The second name is for the Lammers family.

The whole skeleton, put back together, is on exhibit at the Academy of Natural Sciences in Philadelphia, Pennsylvania.

Dodson's work was done, but he worried about the people of Montana. He thought they must feel deprived to have dinosaurs dug up from their land and taken to far-away museums. So he organized one more big effort. With help from lots of people, he was able to get a perfect cast of the original skeleton.

On July 3, 1993, just after the Fourth of July parade and just before the rodeo, Dodson presented the cast to the people of Montana. So now *Avaceratops lammersi* is also on exhibit in the Upper Musselshell Museum.

And that's how Ava came back home to Harlowton, Montana.

The Making of a Fossil

There must have been thousands of dinosaurs of Ava's kind that lived and died but left no trace. It's not easy for an animal to become a fossil.

Millions of animals die in the wild every year. Their flesh is eaten by other animals that we call predators and scavengers, such as lions, hyenas, coyotes, foxes, and vultures. The bones are torn apart and carried away. They are chewed on by big animals and finally by little animals like rats and mice. You can see why so few animals ever become fossils.

To be preserved as a fossil, an animal must die in some special and unusual way so that its bones will be quickly buried. One place this can happen, as it did to Ava, is in the sand and mud of rivers. Of course, animal skeletons usually come apart, and their bones are scattered along the river. We are lucky that Ava's skeleton was buried so quickly that most of it stayed together.

The Lonely Giant Panda

Pandas are hooked on bamboo as their fast food.

The giant panda is a big black-and-white bearlike animal. In the wild it lives only in the mountains of central China. It is a very special animal to the Chinese, and they are worried that it may soon become extinct. Because so little was known about the giant panda, there was a special scientific study reported in 1985.

A first surprise of the report is that in the whole of China there are only about 1,200 wild pandas left. The places where they live, all added up, make an area smaller than the state of New Hampshire. And since people live in the valleys, where land is made into farms, only the upper mountainsides are left for pandas. One special place, high up in the mountains, was chosen for study by a team of scientists. It had eighteen pandas in an area of about fourteen square miles.

Studying pandas is hard work. They like to live in bamboo thickets where even their black-and-white markings cannot be seen from more than thirty feet away. A panda has good ears and a good nose—and it likes to be alone. In a whole year of study, the research team actually saw pandas only thirty-nine times.

How do you study an animal you can't often see? One way was to track them through the woods and look for signs of what they had been doing. Their feces told a lot about what they had been eating. Another way was to trap them and put radio collars on them. That worked for six pandas that came to be the most studied of all. One of the pandas, an adult female, was named Zhen-Zhen.

Zhen-Zhen spent most of her time in a small area only about a half-mile across. Her home range overlapped a little with that of another female, but the two never got close enough to see each other. An adult male, Wei-Wei, also had an overlapping range, but only during the spring mating

season. Tracks in the snow and the records of radio-collared animals told the same story: only rarely did two animals get closer than half a mile apart. In the wild, pandas are real loners.

Beeps from the radio collars also told whether an animal was active or resting. That made it possible to figure out how a panda spends its time. Usually during the course of a day, Zhen-Zhen spent only about a half-hour walking around, ten hours resting, and thirteen hours feeding.

Any playing? Well, not much. There was one account of the tracks left by a young panda in the snow. It had found a clear, snowy slope and acted like a toboggan, belly-slamming downhill. Then it had walked back uphill to do it again. Young pandas in zoos find ways to play. But in the wild there doesn't seem to be much for a panda to do that looks like fun (at least to us).

The life of a panda seems to be spent mostly in feeding. It will eat different kinds of food, including meat, if it gets a

chance. But it lives almost surrounded by one kind of food—bamboo—and it has come to depend almost completely on bamboo for its nourishment. In one way that's good. When a panda wakes up, breakfast is right there. It can reach out for a bamboo stem and start chewing. Its teeth are just right for grinding up bamboo stems. And from the teeth of fossils that have been found, it seems likely that pandas have been living on bamboo for at least the past million years.

The Problems with Bamboo

All that sounds great. But making a living by eating bamboo isn't all peaches and cream. Bamboo is nutritious, all right—if you eat enough. Most of the stuff in bamboo is made of fibers that a panda can't digest. So it turns out that a two-hundred-pound panda needs about thirty pounds of bamboo a day. No wonder that it has to spend most of its time crunching up bamboo in order to get enough to eat.

There is another problem with bamboo. Most of the time it multiplies by new stems that grow up from the roots. Every so often, maybe only once in fifty years, it produces flowers and seeds. When that happens, all the rest of the plant dries up and dies. That's hard on pandas, especially when all the bamboo plants in an area flower together. More than forty pandas starved to death in one area where that happened in 1974.

Dr. George Schaller, one of the directors of the first panda project, has continued his studies in a different area of western China. He has told about his work in a book, *The Last Panda*, written in 1993. It contains more details and ideas that help us think about the panda's problems.

As with some other endangered species, there is a problem with poaching, illegal killing of pandas just for their skins. China as a country has love and respect for the giant panda as its own special animal. But in the western mountains the people are very poor, and panda skins can be sold for a lot of money. Getting the mountain people to help save pandas is a problem yet to be solved.

Pandas and Black Bears

In western China, Dr. Schaller was able to study pandas and the local black bears side by side. Bears eat many different foods, mainly meat, fruits, seeds, and nuts. These are rich in protein and fat. A bear must do a lot of searching for its food, but its foods are very nutritious. In the fall it can eat enough and store up enough fat that it can hibernate through the winter.

The panda doesn't spend much time looking for food. It just plops down in a bamboo thicket and begins crunching. And a panda needs to keep eating most of the time that it is awake. A panda can't eat enough bamboo to build up enough fat to hibernate. So all winter long, even in snowstorms, it must keep crunching bamboo while the bear is curled up sleeping in a hollow log.

Of course, it must be convenient for an animal to have an always-abundant supply of food, even if it is of poor quality. But why has the panda locked itself into such a dependence on bamboo? Dr. Schaller wondered about that, especially since he found many other nutritious plants that the bears liked but the pandas ignore. That was one question for which he could find no answer.

There is more to learn about the giant pandas. But the main part of the story now has been told. Long ago the panda became dependent on just one kind of food. It can live wild only where there is lots of bamboo. Today, people have taken most of that part of the world where it can live. It has no place to go. The giant panda lived on this earth for millions of years before people. I hope we can find a way to help it live here a little longer.

Magnetic Bacteria

Some of the smallest swimmers have compasses.

In science, progress doesn't always go 1-2-3. Some discoveries are unexpected. In fact there is a word for that: serendipity. It has the meaning of accidental discovery. Here is a story of *serendipity*.

A scientist was studying bacteria living in salt marshes on Cape Cod, Massachusetts. He had collected some mud and was looking through his microscope at a speck of mud in a drop of water. Usually such a sample would contain thousands of bacteria, most of them quietly at rest, a few swimming every which way in the drop. He was surprised to see a lot of bacteria all swimming in one direction. At first he thought they might be swimming toward the light from a window, but it was easy to find out that they did not care about light. The mystery was solved when he brought a magnet close to the waterdrop. Then he could "tell" the bacteria which way to go by moving the magnet. If he reversed the magnet, all those bacteria made a U-turn and swam back the other way. Without any magnets around, those bacteria always swam toward the north and downward.

Just to watch a bacterium swimming is an accomplishment. It takes a microscope with 1000x magnification. Even that magnification is not enough to see the tiny whiplike flagellum that propels the bacterium. Swimming bacteria are not very exciting. They never swim very far or very fast, and never seem to go in any special direction. But here they were all swimming together like a school of fish.

These tiny organisms behave as if they had built-in compasses. Our earth is itself a big magnet. So a little magnetic needle that swings freely will line itself up with the big earth magnet to point north and south. When people discovered that idea about a thousand years ago and invented the

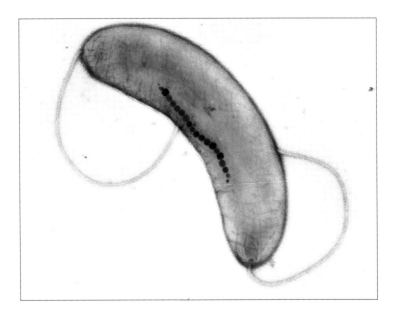

This swimming bacterium—shown here more than 30,000 times larger than actual size—has a chain of dark magnetite particles inside it. These tiny magnets keep the bacterium always swimming toward north.

compass, it became a new high-tech gadget. It made possible navigation on ocean voyages even out of sight of land. After studying some animals that are expert navigators, scientists began to suspect that these animals may have their own ways of sensing the earth's magnetic fields.

Why would bacteria "want" to swim north? It turned out that the kinds of bacteria that do this grow best where there is a low amount of oxygen. And the place to find low oxygen in a salt marsh is down at the bottom, in the mud.

Now we need to know another idea about the magnetism of the earth. The magnetic pole is deep within the earth and near the North Pole. If a compass needle is also allowed to move up and down, it points almost north and also at an angle down toward the magnetic pole. So swimming toward the magnetic pole helps those bacteria swim downward toward where they can live best.

South-Pole Swimmers?

Now if all this is true, there is another question we should ask. What about bacteria in the Southern Hemisphere? To go down, they would need to swim toward the south magnetic pole. So the scientist went to Australia and New Zealand. He found magnetic bacteria there, and sure enough, those bacteria swam toward the south. So it turns out that bacteria from the Northern and Southern Hemispheres swim in opposite directions in a magnetic field.

In pictures taken with the electron microscope, magnetic bacteria showed neat little chains of particles inside. The particles contained the chemical Fe_3O_4. That is the same stuff that makes up the mineral magnetite. So you could say that each of these bacteria has made itself into a compass needle. Bacteria are very tiny one-celled organisms—almost as simple as a living organism can get. So I think it remarkable that some of them can tell about north and south better than I.

The Magnetic Sense

How many creatures have built-in compasses?

Imagine that you are sitting in a canoe on a dark and cloudy night in the middle of a big lake. You are completely lost. You have no idea which way to paddle or where you might get by paddling in any one direction.

While you are worrying about what you might do, think about the many other creatures that would have no problem at all. A long list of animals as different as birds, bees, fish, turtles, and whales would know right off what direction would take them home.

For more than twenty years scientists have been seeking to understand the mystery of this "sixth sense" of direction.

By trying out ideas and solving problems one by one, they are now getting close to an answer.

One idea that is fun to think about is that animals might have a built-in compass. The idea of an animal compass came just from observing animals in nature. Many birds migrate between their summer homes and their winter homes twice a year. Some of them fly for thousands of miles and mostly at night. Experiments have shown that some birds can recognize star patterns. But they can keep on course even under cloudy skies. How can they do that?

The Homing Pigeon

A common bird that does not migrate but is great at finding its way home is the homing pigeon. Not all pigeons are good at finding their way home. Those that can are very good at it and have been widely studied.

One neat experiment was to attach little magnets to the birds' heads. On sunny days that did not fool the pigeons. Evidently they can use the sun to tell direction just as you can. But on cloudy days the pigeons with magnets could no longer find their way. It was as if the magnets were blocking the magnetic sense just as a loud radio can keep you from hearing a call to supper. Similar experiments with the same kind of results were done with honeybees, which also seem to have a special sense of direction.

In spite of the experiments, the idea of an animal compass seemed pretty far out. How would an animal get the magnetic stuff for a compass? As I described in the chapter titled "Magnetic Bacteria," an answer came from an unexpected source. A scientist was studying little rodlike bacteria that all swam together in one direction—north. More study showed that each little bacterium had a chain of dense particles inside. And the particles proved to be magnetite, a magnetic form of iron oxide. They had made themselves into little magnets that could line up with the earth's giant magnet.

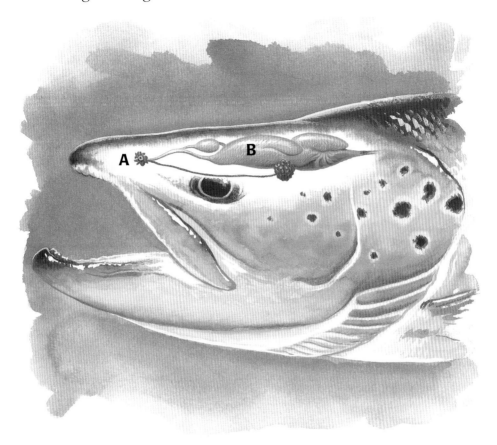

The trout's nose (A) contains particles of magnetite. Nerve fibers (shown in red) start at the nose and come together to form a big nerve that takes magnetic information to the brain (B). This "magnetic sense" nerve is completely separate from the nerve shown in blue, which carries information about smell.

The big news was that a living thing, even a simple little bacterium, can make magnetite. That led to a search to see whether animals might have it. Fortunately, there is a very sensitive instrument, the magnetometer, for detecting tiny amounts of magnetism. By using it, scientists were able to find magnetite in bees, birds, and fish. Except for the bees, the magnetic stuff was always in or close to the brain. The idea of a built-in animal compass began to seem reasonable.

The Trout's Nose

Now a team of scientists in New Zealand have brought us another step closer to understanding the magnetic sense. They found that a freshwater fish, the trout, would respond to a magnetic field. They chose it for further study because they already knew a lot about its nervous system. They found magnetite, all of it located in the fish's nose. That spot has nerve fibers that form a big nerve on its way from the nose to the brain. A change in the magnetic field around the fish set off nerve messages that were carried to the brain. They had pinpointed the location of the trout's magnetic sense. They had found its compass.

This chain of discoveries still has one more step to go. We know now that an animal can have a built-in compass. But we do not know how it works to send nerve messages to the brain. We know how the eye senses light and how the ear senses sound. Now we can look forward to the last chapter about how the animal compass works, how it senses a magnetic field.

The Sharp Eyes of the Falcon

Scientists invented an eye test for a falcon.

We have always supposed that birds of prey, the falcons and hawks and eagles, must have very sharp eyes. They soar above the treetops, sometimes much higher. Then suddenly they fold their wings and swoop down, using their talons to pick up a field mouse or even a grasshopper. They must be able to see small objects even at rather great distances. How well do they really see? Only recently has that been measured in the laboratory. I thought you might like to know how it was done.

What we mean by "sharp eyes" or "good vision" is better said by a technical term, *visual acuity*. It is measured by

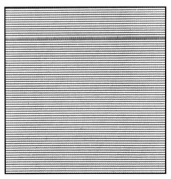

asking the question: From how far away can you distinguish some small object and decide whether or not it is there? Or we can ask the same question in a different way: At some distance, say at two meters or about six feet away, how small an object can you see?

A test of visual acuity that we commonly use is an eye chart. The chart has lines of letters of different sizes and is observed from some distance (perhaps twenty feet). The test is used to find out the smallest-sized letters you can read at that distance. This is a quick and simple way to tell if your eyes are making any big optical errors that could be corrected by eyeglasses. Most young people do not need eyeglasses. But even then there is a limit to the visual acuity of the human eye. No one can see a mouse as far as a mile away.

A Tougher Eye Test

A better test of visual acuity can be made by using a grating. One of these is shown in the square at the upper left corner of this page. At a normal reading distance you can see that it is made from a series of equally spaced white and black bars. Try looking at it from distances farther and farther away. At some distance, you will no longer be able to see separate white and dark bars. They become blurred together. The grating square will look something like the gray square in the upper right corner of page 51. You are past the limit of visual acuity. We also could do the same kind of experiment at just one distance by using different gratings with narrower and narrower light and dark bars.

Now we are ready to talk about a falcon and how its

visual acuity was measured by three scientists at Vanderbilt University. They had a young falcon that they had brought up in the laboratory and treated as a pet. They named it Wulst. They wanted to measure its visual acuity by using gratings. They needed to find some way for Wulst to tell them whether he  could actually see the bars on a grating. To do this they used a common method for testing animals. The idea is that most animals can be taught to play some special kind of game.

First, they taught Wulst to sit on a platform in a small room. On the opposite wall, 1.8 meters (about 6 feet) away, there were two perches. Just above each perch was a small panel for either of two pictures that appeared when a light was turned on. One picture showed a grating with bars like that on page 50. The other picture was exactly the same size and brightness but was just a uniform gray like that on this page.

The next step was to train Wulst to fly from his platform to the perch that had the grating picture, and then return to his platform. When he chose the grating, he got a reward of a small piece of meat as soon as he landed on the perch underneath. It did not take him long to learn the game of choose-the-grating. In about a week he almost always chose the perch under whichever panel showed the grating. And he learned to do this over and over with twenty to twenty-five trials at each session and two sessions each day. The game must have seemed important to Wulst because playing it was about the only way he got fed.

You may be able to guess the next steps. Wulst had learned to play the game by practicing with a coarse grating that had easy-to-see bars. Now the scientists began to use finer gratings with narrower bars. For a long time Wulst

The falcon Wulst belongs to a species with the scientific name *Falco sparverius*.
It is known also as the American kestrel or the common sparrow hawk.

was not fooled. He could still see the separate bars, even when the scientists could not. As the gratings became still finer and the bars still narrower, Wulst suddenly began to fail. When the gratings became very fine, he seemed to be guessing, because he would choose the grating only about half of the time. That meant that his eyes could not see the separate bars. The grating picture and the gray picture looked alike. He had reached the limit of visual acuity of his eyes.

The visual acuity of normal human eyes is well known. Even so, the scientists repeated the whole series of experiments using two different persons with normal eyes. They just looked at two panels from the same distance away and picked out the panel with the grating. But the human subjects were not so good as Wulst. As the gratings became finer, they began guessing much sooner.

Now the scientists had all the information needed to compare the visual acuity of a falcon eye and a human eye. To really see the bars of a grating, the human eye needs bars about 2½ times wider than are needed by the falcon eye. So you can say that the falcon's eye is about 2½ times sharper than yours.

From studies of the structure of the eye, we know what limits its visual acuity. Acuity depends on the size and tightness of packing of little light-sensitive cone-shaped cells in the back of the eye. They send the messages that your brain puts together to tell what you are seeing. In the falcon's eye these light-sensitive cells are smaller and packed together more closely. That explains the greater visual acuity of the falcon. However, having smaller light-sensitive cells is not always an advantage. A smaller cell cannot catch as much light as a bigger one.

You can see that to get its greater visual acuity, a falcon eye may need more light. The scientists thought of this and repeated their experiments with less light on the grating and the gray square. With less light it turned out that the falcon eye was only a little bit sharper than the human eye. It is possible that in even dimmer light, visual acuity of the human eye may be greater than that of a falcon eye.

There are still other characteristics of the eye that allow it to do its job of seeing. I think we should not say that a falcon eye is always better than a human eye. Maybe we can say that for a falcon's way of life, a falcon eye is better than a human eye.

Butterflies That Taste Bad

Does the viceroy taste bad,
or is it just fooling?

Butterflies have always lived dangerously. As they fly around looking for flowers, there are always birds looking for butterflies. For most birds, a butterfly is a tasty snack.

Some kinds of butterflies have solved that problem in a neat way. The body of a monarch butterfly contains chemicals that make it taste bad—so bad that a bird may even vomit if it eats one. That's a great protection for monarch butterflies because birds quickly learn not to eat them.

The second part of this story is about how monarch butterflies get that bad taste. Their eggs are laid on milkweed plants. Their caterpillars grow up eating milkweed, which contains some bitter chemicals. These are called *cardiac glycosides* because they cause vomiting and even heart failure in some animals.

These chemicals protect milkweed because horses, cows, and deer won't eat them. But the monarch caterpillar can. Even when the caterpillar has grown up to be a butterfly, those bitter chemicals are still in its body. They protect the monarch in much the same way that they protect the milkweed plant.

The third part of the story is about the viceroy butterfly. It looks very much like the monarch. But it lives on willows instead of milkweeds, so it doesn't have a supply of those bitter milkweed chemicals in its food. Naturally, scientists have supposed that the viceroy was using a trick. Birds don't eat the viceroy either, and scientists thought the reason was simply that the viceroy looks so much like the monarch.

Lots of animals in nature have come to look alike over thousands of years. They are called mimics. When they are studied, it always turns out that there is some special advantage in being a mimic. Some flies look like honeybees

Viceroy

Monarch

and even buzz around like bees. These flies can't sting, but they are protected because they look like bees that can.

The viceroy butterfly has also been considered a good example of a mimic. It seemed to be protected from being eaten by birds because it was a mimic of the bad-tasting monarch.

But now there is one more part of the story. Two scientists studying butterflies wondered if viceroy butterflies are really bluffing. Do birds avoid eating them just because they look like monarchs?

Tasting Insects

The scientists did some feeding experiments to find out. They used red-wing blackbirds and three kinds of butterflies: monarchs, viceroys, and some swallowtail butterflies. (The blackbirds often eat swallowtails.) The scientists removed the wings and used only the bodies of the butterflies. That way, the birds couldn't see the wing colors.

So how did the taste test come out? The swallowtails "won." All the birds quickly gulped them down. And which ones lost? That was hard to tell. Fewer than half the monarchs were eaten, and even then very slowly, the way you eat something you don't like. But there were almost the same results for viceroys. The birds acted as if both monarchs and viceroys just didn't taste good. Evidently, the viceroys have some way to get their own bad taste.

The results of the taste test were a surprise. The monarchs and viceroys are look-alike mimics all right. Their common color pattern advertises that they both have a bad taste. Viceroys and monarchs both taste bad, and they look very much alike. So it seems likely that both monarchs and viceroys are mimics that help protect each other.

What Happened to the Mammoths?

Eleven thousand years ago,
they disappeared.

You may have heard about the puzzle of what happened to all the dinosaurs. Why did they die out and become extinct way back in the past, about sixty-five million years ago? We're not sure.

Now we also have the puzzle of what happened to the mammoths. This is really a different question, and not just because the mammoths were very different kinds of animals. The record left for us by their bones and fossils says that the mammoths died out only eleven thousand years ago. Compared to the dinosaurs, the mammoths were here not so long ago. People were living on Earth then. One scientist's theory is that people became such good hunters that they killed off all the mammoths.

The Woolly Mammoth

Mammoths were very large animals, about the size of today's elephants. We know most about one particular kind, the woolly mammoth. It had lots of reddish hair and a heavy layer of fat, and it was able to live in cold places like some parts of present-day Alaska and Siberia. Its long curved tusks could have been used to uncover plants under the snow.

A lot of what we know about mammoths comes from three of them—a baby and two adults. These three were preserved in ice in Siberia. They may have been caught in a sudden storm, covered with snow, and frozen into a big block of ice. They became deep-freeze fossils and were perfectly preserved for thousands of years. From the frozen stuff in the animals' stomachs, scientists were even able to find out that the mammoths ate grasses, water plants, and the young shoots of trees.

Eleven thousand years ago mammoths lived in the northern parts of North America. At about the same time, a new people arrived, probably migrating from Asia to Alaska and then southward. They have been called the Clovis hunters because signs of them were first found near Clovis, New Mexico. They did not leave much of a record: some piled-up skeletons of large animals mingled with the stone spear points that were their hunting tools. They seem to have been among the first people who were big-game hunters. They learned to kill buffalo and deer. Even mammoths? It seems so. Two mammoth skeletons have been found with Clovis spear points among their ribs.

How to Hunt a Giant

How did the Clovis people go about the job of hunting mammoths? You may have seen paintings showing almost-naked men throwing stones and spears at a mad-looking mammoth. That kind of scene does not make much sense. Even with stone-pointed spears and with a lot of men working together, attacking a mammoth right out in the open would have been mighty risky.

If they took such big hunting risks, how did people survive? They did not have big teeth or claws, and they were not faster or stronger than their prey. But they were smarter. Being smarter means that they learned all about animals they hunted. You can suppose they learned to dig pits that could be used as traps. They could have learned how to scare those big animals, maybe with fire, and make them run over cliffs or into sticky swamps. Then killing the big animals with spears would not have been so risky. And the scientist's theory would seem more believable.

All this may seem bloody to you. But in those times long ago, people were predators of the animals around them.

A mammoth calf found preserved in ice.

Hunting was a way to make a living. People were becoming successful hunters.

That brings us back to the question we started with: What happened to the mammoths? They disappeared around the time when the Clovis people and probably other people elsewhere were becoming good hunters. Perhaps the scientist is right. Maybe mammoths became extinct because people killed so many. Not everybody believes this, though. Other scientists think the mammoths died off because of a sudden change in the world's weather.

How do we know about times like eleven thousand years ago? Our best method is called radio-carbon dating. For that we need a sample containing carbon that came from some living thing. The amount of radioactive carbon in the sample tells how old it is. Scientists are getting better and better at measuring the ages of samples that way.

As we find more samples left by mammoths and by the Clovis people, scientists will have more pieces of the puzzle and will be able to see if they fit together. I wonder how it will turn out.

BIBLIOGRAPHY

Dolphins Catch a Wave
Williams, T.M., W.A. Friedl, M.L. Fong, R.M. Yamada, P. Sedivy, and J.E. Haun. 1992. Travel at low energetic cost by swimming and wave-riding bottlenose dolphins. *Nature* 355:821-823.

How Cats Purr
Sissom, D.E.F., D.A. Rice, and G. Peters. 1991. How cats purr. *Journal of Zoology* (London) 223:67-78.

Alligators Get Cavities, Too
Ferguson, M.J.W. 1981. Extrinsic microbial degradation of the alligator eggshell *Science* 214:1135-1137.

A Surprising Thing About Alligators
Ferguson, M.J.W., and T. Joanen. 1982. Temperature of egg incubation determines sex in *Alligator mississippiensis. Nature* 296:850-852.

Diving
Kooyman, G.L., and P.J. Ponganis. 1997. The challenge of diving to depth. *American Scientist* 85:530-539.

Kooyman, G.L. *Weddell Seal, Consummate Diver*. Cambridge (England):Cambridge University Press, 1981.

The Dinosaur That Came Home
Dodson, P. 1986. *Avaceratops lammersi*: a new ceratopsid from the Judith River formation of Montana. *Proceedings of the Academy of Natural Sciences of Philadelphia.* 138:305-317.

The Lonely Giant Panda
Schaller, G.B., H. Jinchu, P. Wenshi, and Z. Jing. *Giant Pandas of Wolong*. Chicago:University of Chicago Press, 1985.

Schaller, G.B. *The Last Panda*. Chicago:University of Chicago Press, 1993.

Magnetic Bacteria
Blakemore, R.P. 1975. Magnetotactic bacteria. *Science* 190:377-379.

The Magnetic Sense
Walker, M.M., C.E. Diebel, C.V. Haugh, P.M. Pankhurst, J.C. Montgomery, and C.R. Green. 1997. Structure and function of the vertebrate magnetic sense. *Nature* 390:371-376.

Kirschvink, J.L. 1997. Homing in on vertebrates. *Nature* 390:339-340.

The Sharp Eyes of the Falcon
Fox, R., S.W. Lehmkuhle, and D.H. Westendorf. 1976. Falcon visual acuity. *Science* 192:263-265.

Butterflies That Taste Bad
Ritland, D.B., and L.P. Brower. 1991. The viceroy butterfly is not a batesian mimic. *Nature* 350:497-498.

What Happened to the Mammoths?
Diamond, J. 1986. The mammoth's last migration. *Nature* 319:265-266.

Diamond, J. 1987. The American blitzkrieg: a mammoth undertaking. *Discover* 8: N6, 82-88.

INDEX

Fossilization, process of, 34, 36
Hawk, common sparrow. *See* Falcon.
Kestrel, American. *See* Falcon.
Kooyman, Gerald, 29, 31-32
Lactic acid, 30, 31
Larynx, 15-18
Last Panda, The, 40
Lungs, 29, 32
Magnetic pole, Earth's, 43-44
  Northern Hemisphere, 44
  Southern Hemisphere, 44
Magnetite, 43, 44, 46-48
Magnetometer, 47
Mammoths, 57-61
  Clovis hunters as predators, 60-61
  extinction, theories of, 57-58, 61
  Siberian fossils, 59
  woolly, 58-61
McMurdo Sound, Antarctica, laboratory, 29, 31, 32
Milkweed, 54-55
Mimics (animal look-alikes), 55-56
Muscles, 18, 29-31
Nitrogen, 31
Nitrogen poisoning, 31
Oxygen, 27, 28, 30-32
Oxygen debt, 30-31
Panda, giant, 37-41
  bamboo as food, 40-41
  compared with black bears, 41
  endangered status, 37, 40, 41
  feeding habits, 39-41
  habitat, 37
  numbers remaining, 37
  play activity, 39
  tracking, 38-39
  Wei-Wei, 38-39
  Zhen-Zhen, 38-39
Radio-carbon dating, 61
Schaller, George, 40
Sea lions, 9
Seal, Weddell, 27-32
  blood circulation, 29-30, 32
  diving behavior, 28-32
  diving limits, 28
  lungs, 32
Sea otters, 9
Sugar, breakdown of, 30
Turtles, 23, 45,
Visual acuity, 49-53
  light-sensitive cells, 53
  testing animals, 50-53
  testing humans, 50, 52-53
  Wulst, 51-53
Voice box. *See* Larnyx.
Whales, 28, 45
Williams, Terrie, 9-13